The Mystery of the Zoo Camp

THREE COUSINS DETECTIVE CLUB®

9610

The Mystery of the Zoo Camp

Elspeth Campbell Murphy
Illustrated by Joe Nordstrom

BETHANY HOUSE PUBLISHERS
MINNEAPOLIS, MINNESOTA 55438

The Mystery of the Zoo Camp
Copyright © 1997
Elspeth Campbell Murphy

Cover and story illustrations by Joe Nordstrom

THREE COUSINS DETECTIVE CLUB® and TCDC® are
registered trademarks of Elspeth Campbell Murphy.

Scripture quotation is from the International Children's Bible.

Published by Bethany House Publishers
A Ministry of Bethany Fellowship, Inc.
11300 Hampshire Avenue South
Minneapolis, Minnesota 55438

Printed in the United States of America.

Library of Congress Cataloging-in-Publication Data

Murphy, Elspeth Campbell.
    The mystery of the zoo camp / Elspeth Campbell Murphy.
        p.   cm. — (Three Cousins Detective Club ; 14)
    Summary: A special day camp lets three cousins get a look at
what happens behind the scenes at the zoo, which helps them solve
a mystery involving an escaping pet snake and a missing diamond
ring.
    ISBN 1-55661-852-2
    [1. Zoos—Fiction. 2. Snakes—Fiction. 3. Cousins—Fiction.
4. Mystery and detective stories.] I. Title. II. Series: Murphy,
Elspeth Campbell. Three Cousins Detective Club ; 14.
PZ7.M95316Myt   1996
[Fic]—dc21   96–45912
                                               CIP
                                              AC

ELSPETH CAMPBELL MURPHY has been a familiar name in Christian publishing for over fifteen years, with more than seventy-five books to her credit and sales reaching five million worldwide. She is the author of the best-selling series *David and I Talk to God* and *The Kids From Apple Street Church*, as well as the 1990 Gold Medallion winner *Do You See Me, God?* A graduate of Trinity College and Moody Bible Institute, Elspeth and her husband, Mike, make their home in Chicago, where she writes full time.

Contents

*"What makes a person wise
is understanding what to do.
But what makes a person foolish
is dishonesty."*

Proverbs 14:8

1

Snakes

*T*itus McKay was not the least bit afraid of snakes. He kept well away from the poisonous ones, of course. He knew it would be foolish not to—unless you *absolutely* knew what you were doing. And Titus McKay was nobody's fool. It's just that he didn't see why snakes should be called horrible and creepy—not even the poisonous ones.

Titus thought a lot about animals. He wanted to be a scientist and study them someday. Well, actually, he was already studying animals. And he had decided that a snake was a snake the way a dog was a dog and a bird was a bird. You couldn't *blame* a snake for being a reptile. It just was what it was.

Yes, Titus thought a lot about animals.

And he thought snakes were fascinating. Even beautiful.

His cousins Timothy Dawson and Sarah-Jane Cooper, who were visiting Titus in the city, did not agree with him.

Or rather, Timothy agreed with him a *little* bit. Timothy loved art. And he said he could see where some snakes had pretty designs and colors. But that didn't mean he *liked* them.

Sarah-Jane did not agree with Titus at all. *Not at all.*

Sarah-Jane was not afraid of much—not even spiders and bees. But she positively hated snakes. Couldn't think of one good thing about them. In fact, whenever she felt like giving herself a good scare, she would peek at the snake chart in the encyclopedia. But then she would have to slam the book shut and shove it back on the shelf because her arms got all shivery just looking at pictures of snakes.

Titus knew this about her and had tried pointing out that she was nuts. But Sarah-Jane stuck to her opinion.

Titus's best friend, Derrick, who lived in the same apartment building as Titus, agreed with Timothy. Sure, there were pretty colors and designs. But those pretty colors and designs were on . . . snakes.

Derrick's cousin April, who was visiting, agreed wholeheartedly with Sarah-Jane. Sarah-Jane and April had just met, but Titus had a feeling they were going to agree about everything.

So Titus stood alone in his good opinion of snakes. That didn't bother him.

They were five kids together. A fun kind of mix-up of cousins and friends.

And they were on their way to Zoo Camp.

What could possibly go wrong?

2

City Zoo

The city where Titus lived had a very nice little zoo right in the middle of a beautiful big park. Admission was free, and the zoo was close enough to walk to. So Titus and his parents went there all the time. Titus knew the zoo like the back of his hand. That meant he knew where everything was from seeing it all the time.

Dogs were not allowed in the zoo, so Titus's little dog, Gubbio, had never been there. But whenever Titus came back from the children's zoo where you got to touch the animals, Gubbio sniffed him suspiciously. What were all these peculiar smells? Titus belonged to him, after all. Gubbio didn't like the idea of his people hanging around a lot of strange "dogs."

Titus was on his way to the children's zoo again. But this time it was different. Today Titus and Derrick and their visitors were going to day camp at the zoo. They would get to go behind the scenes to see how the zoo worked. And they would get up close and personal with some of the animals.

April said, "If they try to make me touch a snake, I'm going to call my mama to come get me."

Derrick laughed. "Yeah, right. After the way you whined and whined to get on an airplane all by yourself so you could come visit and go to Zoo Camp? You really think she's going to come get you?"

April pouted—or pretended to. "She would if they try to make me touch a snake!"

"Nobody's going to make us touch a snake," declared Sarah-Jane. She paused. "They won't, will they, Ti?"

Titus groaned. "You two are pathetic, you know that? April's not afraid to get on an airplane all by herself. But she's afraid to touch a snake. S-J will climb on a huge horse and ride

13

without a saddle. But she's afraid to touch a snake. What kind of sense does *that* make?"

"It makes perfect sense," replied Sarah-Jane as April nodded. "And you didn't answer my question, Ti."

Titus groaned again. "No. Nobody's going to make you touch a snake if you don't want to. But why wouldn't you want to? Besides, we happen to know the snake who lives at the children's zoo, don't we, Derrick? He used to live in our building."

"I've met him," admitted Derrick. "But I never held him and played with him the way you did."

"That's true," said Titus, thinking back. "Why was that?"

"He's a snake," said Derrick simply.

Meanwhile, Sarah-Jane was staring at Titus in horror. "You mean all the zillions of times I've visited, there was a snake in your building and I didn't even know it?"

"He's not there now," said Titus reasonably. "He's at the zoo."

"Are there any more snakes in your building?"

"No," said Titus. Then he paused and

smiled sweetly. "That is, not that I know of."

"Does this snake have a name?" asked Timothy before Sarah-Jane got a chance to scream.

Titus hesitated. He had been afraid someone would ask him that.

3

Kah-Yu-Tee-Py

"What?" asked Timothy. "Speak up, Ti. I can't hear you. You're mumbling."

Titus spoke up clearly. "Cutie Pie."

"What?" asked Timothy again, as if he still hadn't heard right.

"Cutie Pie," repeated Titus. "The snake's name is Cutie Pie. He's a python. So it's spelled P-Y instead of P-I-E. And as for the cutie part . . . Well, he *does* have the sweetest little face. . . ."

His cousins stared at him blankly, as if wondering what kind of person could have come up with a goofy name like that.

Titus guessed what they were thinking. "My father named him," he said.

"Ah-hhh!" said Timothy and Sarah-Jane

together. That explained everything. Uncle Richard was always coming up with silly word jokes.

Titus said, "Wait. It gets worse. Cutie Pie is a ball python. And ball pythons come from Africa. So my dad thought he should have an interesting-*looking* name—like some sort of African word. So he spells the name K-A-H—Y-U—T-E-E—P-Y. Kah-Yu-Tee-Py.

"When people see it, they sound it out, because they think it's this strange name they never heard of before. And they don't know what it is until they hear themselves say it out loud. My father and the snake's owner, Greg, think this is hilarious."

Timothy and Sarah-Jane, Derrick and April all shook their heads sadly.

Titus went on, "Greg is an old friend of my parents and me. He's getting married soon, but his fiancée has this 'thing' about snakes."

He paused and looked accusingly at April and Sarah-Jane, who haughtily ignored him.

"Anyway," Titus continued, "Greg's fiancée said it was either her or the snake. So Greg decided Kah-Yu-Tee-Py had to go."

"Ah-*HAH*!" cried Sarah-Jane as if she had

just won an important argument.

Personally, Titus felt Greg had made the wrong decision. But he knew it wouldn't have been polite to tell him so. Sometimes you just had to keep your opinion to yourself. So Titus never said anything when he came over to see Kah-Yu-Tee-Py and help change his water and just hold him all cozy-curled in his arms.

But he had wondered where Kah-Yu-Tee-Py was going to go.

4

One Sweet Little Snake

When Greg was looking for a good home for Kah-Yu-Tee-Py, he had offered him first to Titus.

Titus said he would have to ask his parents.

After all, that was how he had gotten his little dog, Gubbio. Gubbio's original owners had moved overseas where they couldn't take Gubbio with them.

It was a long story how Gubbio ended up with Titus. But his parents had been very understanding about letting him keep the sweet little Yorkshire terrier.

But when it came to letting him adopt a sweet little ball python, his parents wouldn't listen to reason.

Titus had gotten down on bended knees

and begged and pleaded.

"Kah-Yu-Tee-Py is only three—maybe four—feet long, which is practically *tiny* for a python. And he won't get any bigger, which is one reason they make such good pets. Ball pythons *never* get any longer than five—maybe six—feet. I mean, it's not as if I'm asking for a boa constrictor—which is a very nice snake. But, let's face it, they get to be eleven feet long! A ball python is so calm and gentle. And he *knows* me already. And he's *so* pretty! Oh, please, please, please, please, please!"

But it was all to no avail.

Titus's mother had a "thing" about snakes, too. She had once run screaming from a garden hose—something she was still trying to live down.

So his parents didn't say, "Maybe." And they didn't say, "We'll see." They said, "No."

And that was that.

Sure, Titus was disappointed. Who wouldn't be? But his parents pointed out something that Titus had to admit was true. Snakes were great escape artists. No matter how careful you were, there was always a chance the snake could get out of his cage. And even the nicest snake in the world would scare the living daylights out of Gubbio. (Not to mention Titus's mother.) And Kah-Yu-Tee-Py, through no fault of his own, might even mistake Gubbio for food.

Titus agreed that it wouldn't be fair to Gubbio. After all, he was the pet who had gotten there first.

So Kah-Yu-Tee-Py had gone to the zoo. Not to the big reptile house, but to the children's zoo, where you could touch the animals.

That had worked out very well, because the children's zoo had needed a snake the children could touch (if they wanted to). And Kah-Yu-Tee-Py was very tame and used to being handled. He had been hatched in captivity, not taken out of the wild. Greg had had him since he was a baby.

Derrick said what Titus was thinking. "I'm happy for Kah-Yu-Tee-Py. He has a good home. And at least there, at the zoo, he won't be mixed up in any mysteries. Not like he was when he lived in our building. Right, Titus?"

5

The T.C.D.C.

"**M**ystery! What mystery?!" cried Sarah-Jane and Timothy together. "How could you have a mystery without the T.C.D.C.?"

"What's a 'teesy-deesy'?" asked April.

"It's letters," Derrick told her. "Capital T. Capital C. Capital D. Capital C. It stands for the Three Cousins Detective Club. Timothy, Titus, and Sarah-Jane have solved a lot of mysteries. Only, when this thing happened, Timothy and Sarah-Jane weren't here. So I got to help Titus work the case."

"And *I* wasn't here, either!" wailed April. "Why couldn't I have been here then? I *love* mystery books! I've never actually solved a real-life mystery before. But I could have really helped!"

"I doubt it," said Derrick. "The mystery was that we had to find the snake."

April got over her disappointment real fast. She shrugged. "Oh well, then. Forget it."

But Sarah-Jane was staring at Titus and Derrick with a mixture of puzzlement and horror. "What do you mean you had to find the snake? He was right there in his cage, wasn't he? Well, wasn't he? Don't tell me he got *OUT*?!"

"Yes," said Titus thoughtfully. "It was the funniest thing."

"Funny ha-ha? Or funny weird?" asked Timothy.

"Funny weird," replied Titus.

"But we found the snake," Derrick pointed out.

"Yes-s-s," said Titus slowly, sounding a little bit like a snake himself. "But it was the *way* we found him—all curled up like that."

"What do you mean?" asked April.

Titus explained. "A ball python gets its name from the way it acts when it's scared. It tucks its little head under and rolls itself up into a ball and just hopes that the scary stuff will go away."

They were all quiet for a moment, picturing this. Who hadn't felt like doing that at times?

"Oh, poor thing!" murmured Sarah-Jane before she could stop herself.

"Ah-*HAH*!" cried Titus, as if he had just won an important argument.

Sarah-Jane stared at him. *"What?"*

"You were feeling sorry for a snake. Admit it. I heard you. You said, 'Oh, poor thing!' "

Sarah-Jane tried to wriggle out of it. "I did not. I said, 'Hey! Let's sing!' "

But no one—not even April—would let her get away with that.

So Sarah-Jane said, "OK. OK. I admit it. I felt sorry for a snake. So what happened anyway? What was Kah-Yu-Tee-Py so scared of?"

"*That*," replied Titus. "Is exactly what *I'd* like to know."

6

The Great Escape

*T*itus explained what had happened. He said, "Somehow Kah-Yu-Tee-Py got out of his cage. It's not that he didn't *like* his cage. Greg had it all fixed up as a nice big terrarium. Ball pythons like to climb. So Kah-Yu-Tee-Py had his branch to climb on. And all snakes like to hide, so he had his little hollow log. And he had his water dish and a couple of nice plants. And it was partly sunny and partly shady. Just right.

"But if there's any little opening, a snake will go through it, because that's just what snakes do. He had gotten out once before when Greg hadn't latched the cover on right. After that, Greg always made sure it was shut tight."

"Then how did Kah-Yu-Tee-Py get out again?" squeaked Sarah-Jane, who really, *really* wanted to know.

Greg's fiancée, Julie, had asked the same question in exactly the same way. She had stopped by at the worst possible moment when Greg and Derrick and Titus were taking the place apart looking for the python.

Derrick answered Sarah-Jane. "Greg said he must have forgotten to latch the cover again."

"Yes, that's what he said," agreed Titus. "But he didn't say it like he meant it. He said it like that was the *only* explanation. But he didn't sound like he thought it was a *good* explanation. Do you know what I mean?"

Everyone nodded.

Titus went on. "The *first* time Kah-Yu-Tee-Py got out, Greg and I found him stretched out on Greg's favorite chair. The leather was warm from the sun coming in the window. And there was Kah-Yu-Tee-Py just basking away. It was really cute!"

Sarah-Jane and April looked at each other and shuddered. They were both beginning to like Kah-Yu-Tee-Py a little bit from what they had heard of him. But not *that* much.

"But the *next* time," said Titus, "Greg and Derrick and I found Kah-Yu-Tee-Py all rolled up in a ball behind the couch. Something had scared him, all right."

7

The Rescue

*J*ulie hadn't stayed around to help. So the three guys had pulled the couch out away from the wall.

Then it was up to Titus.

Titus had a way with animals that was kind of hard to explain. They would come to him when they wouldn't go to anyone else. Partly it was that he was very calm around them and very patient.

So he had sat down beside the little snake-ball. Titus knew he could have actually rolled Kah-Yu-Tee-Py across the room like that. He had read that about ball pythons, although he had never seen it happen. But he didn't think it would be right to try it out on Kah-Yu-Tee-Py.

Instead, Titus just rested his hands on Kah-Yu-Tee-Py so the snake could feel the warmth. He talked gently to him—even though Titus knew the snake couldn't hear him the way people hear. Snakes just feel sound vibrations.

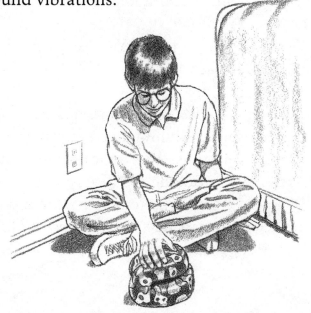

But something got through to Kah-Yu-Tee-Py, because he had begun to relax and un-wind—literally.

Then Titus held him on his lap for a while until he thought maybe Kah-Yu-Tee-Py had dozed off. You could never tell with snakes. They have no eyelids. So they look pretty much the same all the time. You could be talking away to them, thinking they look so interested in what you have to say. Then you'd remember that they can't hear you and are probably sound asleep anyway. It's always hard to tell what a snake is thinking. Or if it's thinking anything at all.

Titus had carried Kah-Yu-Tee-Py back to his cage, and that was that.

Or was it?

Somehow Titus didn't think so.

Derrick said, "I know there are some unanswered questions. But at least we found Kah-Yu-Tee-Py. So the mystery got at least partly solved. That's better than we did with the other mystery. It never got solved at all."

8

The Other Mystery

"*T*he *other* mystery! What other mystery?!" cried Sarah-Jane and Timothy together.

"Well, that happened right about the time Kah-Yu-Tee-Py got out," said Titus. "Julie came back after we got Kah-Yu-Tee-Py back in his cage. She was still pretty upset about him getting out. But then Greg realized that he had lost Julie's diamond engagement ring. And she hadn't even seen it yet."

Sarah-Jane and April gasped in horror. There were some things too awful for words.

Timothy said, "Wow. This guy Greg has a hard time holding on to things, doesn't he? You know, little things: Pythons. Diamonds."

"He almost had a hard time holding on to his fiancée," said Derrick. "She was not a happy camper. First the snake. Then the ring. It had belonged to Greg's grandmother. And it was *very* valuable. The ring, I mean. Not the snake."

"Well, duh," said April.

"What did they *do*?" asked Sarah-Jane, who was just starting to get her voice back.

"They looked high and low," said Titus. "Derrick and I helped. Julie wouldn't go near the snake's cage, so Greg took that end of the room. We just helped where we could. But then we had to go home for supper.

"Greg came over later and told my parents and me the rest of it. Greg's roommate came home while they were still looking for the ring. He's gone a lot. I don't think I've ever actually met him. I think his name's Dave. Anyway, Greg and Julie couldn't help wondering if maybe Dave knew something about the ring. But they didn't want to ask him.

"I don't think Greg likes him all that much. And Dave didn't like living there. He said he was scared of Kah-Yu-Tee-Py all the time.

"Anyway, Dave must have guessed that Greg and Julie kind of suspected him. So he insisted that all three of them search his room.

And he emptied his pockets and everything. It was all very embarrassing. And they didn't find the ring.

"So then Dave made this big deal about giving Greg his apartment key and moving out. He didn't have that much stuff. And he said he had been planning to leave anyway because of being scared of the snake."

"Wow!" said Timothy. "That's quite a story."

"So then what happened?" asked April.

Titus said, "So then Julie took it all out on Kah-Yu-Tee-Py and said it was either him or her. And that's when Greg had to find a new home for him."

"No, no, no, no, no!" wailed April. "Not what happened to the snake. We know what happened to the snake. What happened to the *RING*?"

"Oh, that," said Derrick. "They never found it."

9

Mrs. Dixon

*T*itus said, "Greg was lucky the zoo had an opening for a python. Sometimes people get snakes for pets and then for some reason they can't keep them. But snakes can live a long, long time. So you've got to find a place where they can stay.

"My mother knows this lady, Mrs. Dixon, who's a docent at the zoo. And she put in a good word for Kah-Yu-Tee-Py."

"What's a docent?" asked April.

"It's someone who leads tours at a zoo or a museum," said Derrick.

And Titus added, "Or sometimes the do-cent will stay in one place with something to show. And the people will gather around to see it up close." He looked at Sarah-Jane and April and tried to sound casual. "Why, who knows what she'll have out for the children to touch? Maybe a snake."

Sarah-Jane and April backed away a little as if Titus might pull a snake out of his pocket. Which he never would. Because it wouldn't be fair to the snake.

"It was very nice of Mrs. Dixon to help find a home for Kah-Yu-Tee-Py," said Sarah-Jane in her most ladylike voice.

Titus had to agree. He said, "She even printed up a sign with Kah-Yu-Tee-Py's name on it. Spelled just the way my dad and Greg dreamed up.

"Greg said it was all very decent of her. And my *dad* said—are you ready for this?—'Mrs. Dixon is a decent docent.' "

Everyone groaned. What else could you do?

Timothy patted Titus on the shoulder sympathetically. "It just never ends, does it?"

Titus shook his head.

But there was no time to say any more. They had reached the zoo and were caught up in a crowd of excited kids all wearing Zoo Camp T-shirts. It felt really good to belong.

"Neat-O!" said Timothy.

"So cool!" said Sarah-Jane and April to-gether.

"EX-cellent!" said Derrick.

"Beyond EX-cellent!" said Titus.

10

Zoo Camp

Zoo Camp was being held in the children's zoo. There was a big room where the cages were and a smaller meeting room off to the side. Zoo Camp kids were supposed to report to the meeting room. And to get there, they would have to pass the animals' cages.

Titus wondered if the python would be out yet. Animals are usually kept "off-exhibit" when they first come to the zoo. This gives them time to get used to a new place before all the people come to see them.

Titus was looking forward to seeing his python-friend again.

Timothy said, "So—do you think Kah-Yu-Tee-Py will recognize you?"

"Maybe," said Titus. "Snakes are highly

intelligent, you know." He paused for a moment and thought about this. "Well, maybe not *highly* intelligent. But they're smart enough, I guess. Some people think snakes recognize familiar humans. And some people don't. It's hard to tell with snakes."

But it wasn't hard to tell which was Kah-Yu-Tee-Py's cage. A group of kids had already gathered around saying, "Oooo! A snake! A snake! Look at the snake!"

Kah-Yu-Tee-Py was getting more attention than any other animal. Titus couldn't help feeling jealous of the other kids being there. He knew Kah-Yu-Tee-Py wasn't *his* snake. But still . . . It sort of felt like he was. . . . How could you help loving that sweet little face and wishing you had a python of your very own? Titus tried to snap out of it. At least Kah-Yu-Tee-Py had a good home.

This cage was bigger than the one he had had in Greg's apartment. But the zoo had kept his stuff—his branch and his hollow log and his water dish—and added some more plants. So maybe Kah-Yu-Tee-Py didn't even know that he had moved. It was hard to tell with snakes.

Mrs. Dixon (the decent docent) was there,

keeping the kids from tapping on the glass.

Mrs. Dixon was a retired science teacher, and she didn't have the slightest "thing" about snakes. She was used to handling them.

She was used to handling kids, too.

She said she would get Kah-Yu-Tee-Py out so that everyone could see him up close. But not until they were all in the meeting room. Sitting cross-legged on the floor. No pushing. No shoving. No loud talking.

Mrs. Dixon was a very nice person. But she was also a no-nonsense kind of person, who was more worried about you scaring the snake than the snake scaring you.

When everyone was settled, Mrs. Dixon came into the meeting room with Kah-Yu-Tee-Py and started telling about him.

Titus looked around for April and Sarah-Jane. They were sitting as far back in the circle as they could get without actually being out the door.

Titus was just about to turn back toward Mrs. Dixon when something caught his eye. It was something through the door to the other room where the animals' cages were. And it was something very odd.

11

Something Odd

W hat Titus saw was a young man about Greg's age. There was nothing odd about the young man's appearance. And at first glance what he was doing didn't seem odd either.

He was peering intently into one of the animal cages. Nothing strange about that. In fact, Titus always felt that the best way to visit the zoo was to take your time and look—really look—at the animals. Titus had trained himself to do just that. Studying animals the way he did helped him to notice people, too. That came in handy with detective work!

And that's why Titus noticed something odd: The cage the young man was looking into was Kah-Yu-Tee-Py's.

But, of course, Kah-Yu-Tee-Py wasn't in

his cage. He was in the meeting room. At this moment, he was curled around Mrs. Dixon's arm, excitedly flicking his tongue in and out at the Zoo Camp kids. He wasn't being rude. He was gathering particles from the air that told him what was out there. It was sort of like being able to smell with your tongue as well as your nose.

Titus looked from Kah-Yu-Tee-Py back to the big room where the cages were. So—if Kah-Yu-Tee-Py wasn't in his cage—what was that guy looking at? Sometimes snakes could be hard to see because their colors blended right in with the ground. That was true in the wild. And the zoo always tried to make its cages look like a little bit of the outdoors.

But even with camouflage, Titus thought, it wouldn't take you that long to see there was no snake in there. So what was the guy looking at? What could be so interesting about branches and plants, a water dish, and a hollow log?

All this flitted through Titus's mind pretty quickly. At the same time, he realized he had seen the man before. But he couldn't place him.

Titus nudged Timothy and Derrick. "Do you recognize that guy back there in the other room? The one looking in Kah-Yu-Tee-Py's cage?"

Timothy said, "Why is he looking in Kah-Yu-Tee-Py's cage if Kah-Yu-Tee-Py isn't there?"

"That's what I'd like to know," said Titus. "Do you recognize him from anywhere?"

"No," said Timothy. "I've never seen him before."

But Derrick said, "Sure. I've seen him. Didn't he used to live in our building?"

12

Snake Line

*A*s soon as Derrick said that, Titus realized who the man was. He had even met him once. But that had been quite a while ago, and the man had been on his way out. He was gone a lot. So what was he doing *here*? And why would someone who said he was afraid of Kah-Yu-Tee-Py be looking for him so intently?

But before Titus could tell Timothy and Derrick what he was thinking, Mrs. Dixon cleared her throat. She looked sternly at the group in a way that meant, There's too much talking going on in here!

Titus hardly ever got in trouble. And he didn't want to start now. He turned around to pay attention. But he couldn't help glancing back just one more time. The man was gone.

Or at least Titus couldn't see him.

Mrs. Dixon asked who would like to help her hold Kah-Yu-Tee-Py.

Titus's hand shot straight up in the air as if it had a mind of its own. Since he was the first one with his hand up, Mrs. Dixon picked him. Also, she knew that Titus and Kah-Yu-Tee-Py were old friends.

Certainly Kah-Yu-Tee-Py went to Titus right away. So maybe he did recognize him as that nice kid from the apartment building. Who knew?

While Titus and Mrs. Dixon held Kah-Yu-Tee-Py, the other kids got to file by and touch the python. (But no one *had* to.)

Some of the kids had been under the impression that snakes are wet and slippery. They seemed surprised to find out that a snake's skin is dry and feels something like leather.

Sarah-Jane and April had managed to be the absolutely last two people in line.

That hadn't been easy.

Two other girls and at least three boys had wanted to be last, too.

There had been a bit of a scuffle.

But Mrs. Dixon had cleared her throat.

And the scared-of-snakes people had gotten in line with everyone else. Sure, pythons were scary. But you didn't mess with Mrs. Dixon.

Neither Sarah-Jane nor April quite got up enough nerve to touch Kah-Yu-Tee-Py. But they did look at him sort of up close. And—for them—that was really something.

Another docent began dividing the group into teams. Titus was going to be on the same team as Timothy, Derrick, April, and Sarah-Jane. But for now he was excused to help Mrs. Dixon with Kah-Yu-Tee-Py.

Titus carried Kah-Yu-Tee-Py out of the meeting room and across the main room.

A couple of little boys saw him and yelled, "Mommy! That big boy has a snake! That big boy has a snake!"

But the little kids weren't the only ones paying attention to him.

Out of the corner of his eye Titus was looking to see if that guy was still there.

He was.

Without being at all obvious about it, Titus moved to the other side of Mrs. Dixon.

He may have recognized the guy. But he didn't want the guy to recognize him.

But why he felt that way—Titus wasn't sure.

13

Behind the Scenes

Mrs. Dixon unlocked a door that led to a small round room. Usually only zoo keepers and docents were allowed in there. But this week Titus was a Zoo Camp kid, so he got to go behind the scenes.

All around the walls of the room were more doors. These were smaller than the door they had come through. These smaller doors opened into the animals' cages.

When Mrs. Dixon opened a nearby door, Titus realized he was standing at the back of Kah-Yu-Tee-Py's cage. He was looking out at the people in the big room. This was the animals' point of view.

Kah-Yu-Tee-Py's busy little tongue flicked in and out, taking it all in. *Now* where was he?

Oh, yes. Here was his stuff. He was home again. After his Big Adventure at Zoo Camp.

Titus carefully put Kah-Yu-Tee-Py down. The python seemed to have a favorite corner already. He crawled over there and curled up. Not in his scared way. This was his relaxed, go-to-sleep way.

Titus knew that ball pythons sleep during the day and are mostly awake at night. And suddenly he understood his mother's point of view. If you had a "thing" about snakes, it would be hard to sleep knowing there was a snake in the house, who was wide awake. Even if he couldn't get out of his cage.

Except—sometimes snakes *did* get out. Kah-Yu-Tee-Py had. Twice. The first time had been Greg's mistake. Titus was sure of that. But the second time? Titus wasn't convinced.

Mrs. Dixon closed the door to Kah-Yu-Tee-Py's cage and locked it. At least Everybody's Favorite Python couldn't get out of there. And no one could get in.

Mrs. Dixon and Titus washed up at a sink in the room. It was always a good idea to wash before and after you handled animals.

They were just drying their hands when

there came a sudden, loud knock at the people door. It was so unexpected that both Titus and Mrs. Dixon jumped.

"Who could that be?" she muttered as she went to see.

Titus had a pretty good idea who it could be. And he was right.

It was the man he had recognized. The one who was so interested in Kah-Yu-Tee-Py's cage.

Titus turned away before the man could see him and pretended to be busy with something. But actually, he was listening hard.

"Oh, hello," the man said to Mrs. Dixon. He was trying to sound friendly and casual. But it sounded phony. "I saw you come in here, and I wondered if I could join the tour."

"Tour? What tour?" asked Mrs. Dixon, firmly blocking his way. "This room is not open to the public, young man."

"Oh! Oh, it isn't? Sorry. My mistake!" And he quickly left the building.

Mrs. Dixon was nobody's fool.

"How very odd!" she said to Titus. "I have a feeling that young man is up to no good."

"He's up to something, all right," agreed Titus. "I just don't know what."

14

The Gorillas' Yard

*W*hen Titus got back to the meeting room, he saw that almost everyone had gone off already. There was just one other team and his own team waiting for him with a docent.

As soon as she saw him, Sarah-Jane burst out, "Oh, Ti! Ti! Guess what! They're going to put us in the gorilla yard!"

Titus realized he must have looked pretty alarmed, because everyone laughed.

"The gorillas won't be out when we're there," Timothy assured him.

The docent explained that in the wild the gorillas hunt through grass and bushes for things to eat. It was called foraging. The zookeepers wanted the gorillas to have the same experience in captivity. So they put out fruit and vegetables for the gorillas to find.

Titus got so excited about helping with this that he almost forgot his news. But on the way to the great ape house, he was able to talk to his fellow detectives.

He said, "Derrick, you know that guy that I recognized? Well, I got a better look at him. And I realized who he was. Dave. Greg's old roommate."

"Of course!" cried Derrick. "That's who he was! I couldn't place him at first."

"What was he doing here?" asked Timothy. "Although—I suppose anyone can come to the zoo if he wants to."

"I think he was here for a reason," said Titus. "The way he was looking at Kah-Yu-Tee-Py's cage. Just looking and looking."

"Dave told Greg he was afraid of Kah-Yu-Tee-Py," said Sarah-Jane.

"I know," said Titus. "But was he really? He saw me go into this little room carrying a four-foot python. Then he knocks on the door and wants to come in, too. Is that something that someone who's afraid of snakes would do?"

"No way!" cried Sarah-Jane and April to-gether.

"But why would you lie about a thing like that?" asked April.

Titus said, "The answer to that is—I have no idea."

By this time they had reached the great ape house, and the docent led them out into the grassy yard. The gorillas couldn't get out yet, because the door leading to the yard was shut. The kids had the place to themselves.

The yard was actually a grassy hill sur-rounded by glass walls. That way, the people could see in, and the gorillas couldn't get out.

All up and down the hill there were ropes and ladders and swings for the gorillas to play on. It was sort of like a playground for kids, only bigger.

But the Zoo Camp kids weren't there to play. They had a job to do.

The docent gave them each a little bag of fruits and vegetables and told them to hide the food for the gorillas to find later. The hiding places had to be not too easy, but not too hard. It was like hiding Easter eggs for little kids.

"You know—" said April later when they

were headed back to the children's zoo. "If you had to hide something important, the gorillas' yard would be a pretty good place. You'd have to put it where gorillas couldn't get it. But then no one else could get it, either. Because, who's going to go in there when the gorillas are out?"

Titus stopped dead in his tracks and stared at her. "That's it," he said.

15

The Python's Secret

*I*t took a while—quite a while—to explain to his mother on the phone why she and his father and Greg had to meet them at the zoo.

Zoo Camp was over at lunchtime. And the cousins and Derrick and April were HUNGRY. But there was something they had to do.

Titus explained it some more when his parents and Greg got there. He said, "All along, Derrick and I thought there were two separate mysteries. One was about Kah-Yu-Tee-Py: How did he get out of his cage, and what scared him? The other mystery was about Julie's ring: What happened to it?

"But there weren't two separate mysteries. There were two parts of the *same* mystery.

"When April said that about hiding something in the gorillas' yard, it hit me. What if someone was afraid of snakes? Where's the one place you could hide her ring that she would never, *ever* look?"

Mrs. Dixon took it right in stride when Titus explained that they would have to search Kah-Yu-Tee-Py's stuff.

But it made Titus nervous. What if he were wrong? How embarrassing!

But Titus wasn't wrong.

On the inside roof of Kah-Yu-Tee-Py's hollow log, Greg found a piece of sticky brown packing tape. Stuck to the tape on the other side was a tiny paper packet. And inside the packet was a diamond ring.

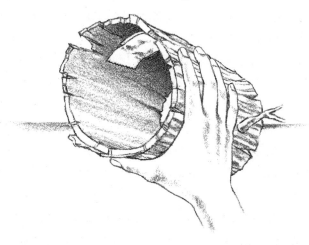

"I knew that young man was up to no good!" said Mrs. Dixon.

Greg said, "I'm not surprised Dave stole the ring. I suspected him right away."

"He knew you would," said Timothy. "That's why he made you search his stuff. He knew you wouldn't find the ring. He had already hidden it in Kah-Yu-Tee-Py's cage."

"That's what I don't understand," said Greg. "How could Dave hide the ring in Kah-Yu-Tee-Py's cage if he was afraid of snakes?"

"Dave *wasn't* afraid of snakes," said Titus. "He only said that to throw you off. Did he ever say anything before about Kah-Yu-Tee-Py being in the apartment?"

"Now that you mention it, no," said Greg. "He just ignored him."

Titus pointed to his mother, Sarah-Jane, and April, who were sitting as far away from Kah-Yu-Tee-Py's cage as they could get without actually being out the door.

"People who have a 'thing' about snakes can't live in the same apartment with them," he said.

Greg nodded. "I haven't been very understanding about Julie. No wonder she got so upset when Kah-Yu-Tee-Py got out." He paused as he realized something. "That was the first mystery, wasn't it? Kah-Yu-Tee-Py must have gotten out when Dave hid the ring."

"Right," said Titus. "He was messing around in the cage. Who knows? He might even have shoved Kah-Yu-Tee-Py out of his log. So when Dave didn't fix the latch right, Kah-Yu-Tee-Py got out of there and went away and hid."

"Poor thing," said Sarah-Jane before she could stop herself. Then she quickly added, "Dave probably didn't even know Kah-Yu-Tee-Py had gotten out. By the time he came back, Titus had Kah-Yu-Tee-Py all calmed down and back in his cage. So Dave had no way of knowing that Julie had said the snake had to go. He thought he could just come back and get the ring whenever you were gone."

"He made a big deal about giving you his key," said Derrick.

"But keys can be copied," said April. "He probably had another one."

Titus said, "It must have been a big shock to him to discover that Kah-Yu-Tee-Py and his log were gone. He must have guessed he had gone to the zoo. Kah-Yu-Tee-Py's name tag told him he had guessed right. He could even see the hollow log. But there was no way to break into the cage."

"No, indeed!" said Mrs. Dixon.

The little restaurant in the zoo had the best hot dogs in town, and Greg treated everyone to lunch. (Not Kah-Yu-Tee-Py. He had swallowed a rat only last week, and he still wasn't hungry. He just curled up and went to sleep.)

When the cousins finally got home, Gubbio went crazy sniffing, sniffing, sniffing. What were all these strange smells? Where had these people been?

"It's python and gorilla," Titus told him. "But don't worry. When it comes to Yorkshire terriers, you're the only one for me!"

The End

Series for Young Readers*
From Bethany House Publishers

★ ★ ★

THE ADVENTURES OF CALLIE ANN
by Shannon Mason Leppard
Readers will giggle their way through the true-to-life escapades of Callie Ann Davies and her many North Carolina friends.

★ ★ ★

BACKPACK MYSTERIES
by Mary Carpenter Reid
This excitement-filled mystery series follows the mishaps and adventures of Steff and Paulie Larson as they strive to help often-eccentric relatives crack their toughest cases.

★ ★ ★

THE CUL-DE-SAC KIDS
by Beverly Lewis
Each story in this lighthearted series features the hilarious antics and predicaments of nine endearing boys and girls who live on Blossom Hill Lane.

★ ★ ★

RUBY SLIPPERS SCHOOL
by Stacy Towle Morgan
Join the fun as home-schoolers Hope and Annie Brown visit fascinating countries and meet inspiring Christians from around the world!

★ ★ ★

THREE COUSINS DETECTIVE CLUB®
by Elspeth Campbell Murphy
Famous detective cousins Timothy, Titus, and Sarah-Jane learn compelling Scripture-based truths while finding—and solving—intriguing mysteries.

* (ages 7–10)